John and Santa

John and Santa
The Cowboy Shirt

a novella
by
John Passfield

Rock's Mills Press
Rock's Mills, Ontario • Oakville, Ontario
2022

Published by
Rock's Mills Press
www.rocksmillspress.com

Author's Note: The December 2021 meeting of the Second Thursday Book Discussion Group took place in a meeting room at St. John the Divine Church in Cayuga, Ontario, on Thursday, December 9, in the second year of the Covid 19 pandemic, during the surge of the Omicron variant of the virus.

Cover design: Craig Passfield
Cover illustration: An elementary-school photograph of John Passfield

For information about this book, including bulk and retail orders and permissions requests, please contact the publisher:
customer.service@rocksmillspress.com

Author's website: www.johnpassfield.ca

John and Santa

Chapter 1

Driving home from the meeting. A very enjoyable afternoon. The topic, of course, was Christmas. It's our December topic each year. Nice to get together at the restaurant. Then the presentations and discussion at the meeting-room at the church. Fifteen is a pretty good number – what with Covid precautions and all. No agenda – just whatever one cares to say.

Hearing Christmas carollers in the yard.

It's the time of year for memories. We all talked about Christmases-past. I told them about my son and the reindeer teeth. And the one about the boy with the Santa-beard. Everybody had a story or two to tell. Smaller gatherings now with the Covid pandemic. Christmas-time is more for kids than for adults.

Two flames were created

A person driving home in a car.
A dream that might not be a dream.
Thinking in non-human terms.

on the day

Did this story actually happen?
Should this be classed as 'fiction' or not?

Did you get Santa to sign a release?

the world was made.

In Asia Minor, near modern Demre, Turkey.
The custom of giving gifts and sweets to children.
Drawings in Harper's Weekly.

Working on polishing my novel. Be nice to get home and get back to work. Nice to finish it before the end of the year. Nothing nicer than having a complete rough-draft to read. Always searching for better words. I get up every morning and read it again and again. Nice to have a choice of future topics. Soon I'll get the urge to start the whole process again.
In his master's steps he trod.
Thinking about Charles Dickens. Almost Christmas time again. How can I call myself a writer? Look what Dickens was able to do. He wrote a book that created Christmas as we know it today.

He was a little boy. He was watching the Christmas concert. He had to go to the washroom.

Driving home from our Christmas book-discussion meeting.
Thinking of all the topics that we discussed.

He had a theory
that the books
are all about us.

A little less painful - searching for the exit - a world-
wide tour - take a close look - each one sees itself - be-

*yond the known horizons - picture the scene - patterns
of potential meaning - started with a simple question
- no past and no future.*

That there is
no such thing as
'art for art's sake'
at all.

*It was the story
of an ancient Greek.*

I wasn't sure what topic to take to the meeting this
time. I knew what I wanted to talk about but not which
carol I wanted to read. A vague memory of presenting
Silent Night a couple of years ago. The idea that the carol is presented entirely in character and scene. A Christmas carol as a film – a series of images – as visual as
a dream. The kind of thing that we used to colour in
Sunday School.

Putting presents under a Christmas tree.

Hard to believe how it could have happened. About
my mom and the cowboy shirt. How old would I have
been about that time? It was a mystery that would have
baffled Sherlock Holmes.

*The explorer
was crawling
on his belly.*

That art is a level of the mind –
a level of thought about ourselves
and our experience –
that is so far down in our heads

that we are not always aware.

*Year after year
the Krampus
requested a meeting.*

It had been a difficult evening. Oh it was fun until it was time to go to bed. Only a few things left to do on Christmas Eve.

That art is the dredging-up of the images
from the mind's deep core
and arranging them on the table
for all to see
and think about
in concrete form.

*The legend of Sinterklaas.
Portly, jolly, white-bearded.
Illustrator Haddon Sundblum.*

Driving home from the meeting. Can't wait to get back to work. *Shakespeare and Cleopatra.* Plenty of thoughts as I polish each page. How one of the main characters is real and one is not. But then, the complications — both are real and both are not. Both of them have been created by me.
Let nothing you dismay.
I'll have to get it down from my shelf. I haven't read that book for years. Christmas goose and the giving of presents. Christmas cheer and a blazing yule log. Does Dickens ever mention Santa Claus?

They had gone – Dad and his four-year old – to buy

a present for Mom. And something for the little brother would be nice as well. To the lady's section of a local department store.

Thinking of the idea-structure of the Dickens novella.

A guide presents the main character with various scenes.

Whether a film or a painting,
or a sculpture or a vase,
or a poem or a poetic novel
or a poetic play.

Had never seen actual snow - affected by the process - or to be kinder - significant imagery - they might be gone - pinpoint the minute - exist in different zones - the secrets of the universe - forces in the world - the shade of the sail.

That art is the everyday image-process
that ebbs and flows
like magma
in the depths of the brain.

Clutch the toys
you receive at Christmas.

One presentation was of family postcards – with Christmas greetings from as far back as 1905. Another one was on the Krampus – I had no idea what it was. The one I decided to do was *King Wenceslas*. There's a million ways to think about Christmas-time. I'd love to write a Christmas novel if I had an idea.

Merry Christmas to you.

I suppose I would be about seven – or eight – or nine. Memories mingle and interlayer. *Rudolph the Red Nosed Reindeer* – by Gene Autry – was a brand-new song at that time. The family would gather at our house for dinner. Grandpa would light the Christmas cake. I'd be glancing at all the presents under the tree.

No one

Advertisements which feature Santa Claus.
A person with a head full of thoughts.
A theory of what is outside the outside.

has ever

What do you know of the story of the Krampus?
Is it true that he and Santa were twinned at birth?
Shouldn't that be the idea-angle that you pursue?

left the universe.

But even that is ambivalent. Both of them have been created – but only partially by me. They were both created before I came on the scene. Then they re-created themselves, as much as anybody can. Cleopatra re-created Cleopatra – Shakespeare re-created himself. Then Shakespeare re-created her to suit his purposes. And then I came along and re-created them both again.
The hopes and fears of all the years.
Mom searched and searched in the cupboards. It was a mystery for all of time. It was the present that I never received. But here's the thing that's even more baffling. There's a photograph of me in a cowboy shirt.

Chapter 2

Well, welcome to my sleigh. I get a firm grip on the edge of the seat. I can tell that you're quite surprised. The breeze is brisk but not too forceful. I assume you are quite familiar with who I am. I glance around and we are miles above the ground. I never know how these visits are scheduled. He takes one hand away from the reins. Permit me to introduce myself. He offers his hand in his glove. I hold out one of my hands and tighten the other one, firmly, on the sleigh. Welcome along on the voyage. I place my hand in his. After this, there'll be no more need for formality. If you are wondering, John – my name is Santa Claus.

All is calm, all is bright.

The hand is quite firm in mine. Why thank you – my name is John, but you seem to know that already. The breeze is actually pleasant, though we're miles above the earth. This is all quite a surprise. I didn't come of my own accord. I have this urge to count the reindeer. How many did it say in the poem? I know, of course, who you are. Everyone knows about Santa Claus. His eyes seem to hold me. Would it seem to be an impoliteness if I looked around?

One was

Two people flying in a sleigh.
The makings of a charming little book.
A Godmother who doesn't know her child.

a bright

Read a lot of books in your time?
Enough to fill up sixty years?
Reading every kind of book that has caught your eye?

flame.

Raised him to be a devout Christian.
His feast day is December 6.
Red coat, white fur collar and cuffs.

The Butcher left a butcher-knife and the Baker left a loaf of bread at the scene of the crime, said the detective.

He comes in human flesh to dwell.

I was driving my car, the last I remember. Going home from a meeting in town. We had talked a lot about Christmas – it's December, after all. I was thinking about Christmas carols – about how real they seem to be. They are images that imprint themselves on our minds. I always thought that you were an image – a myth – a story – a tale. And here I am sitting beside you in your sleigh. Images have a power – they can arise and take over the mind. Hope I'm not falling asleep as I'm driving along in my car.

Beside the washroom was the tea-counter. The ladies were serving cookies and tea. A lady was getting a cup of tea to drink.

Suddenly finding myself riding in a flying sleigh.
Knowing in a twinkle that it must be St. Nick.

There are pages floating above my head! I'm sitting here in my reading chair! I have just completed a novel! I am wondering what to write next! I have my pen but the pages are floating away!

Couldn't know the rules - i am the work of art - might not be a dream - a bit of a bump - responding to its life-experience - i missed seeing them - carefully balancing the cup - a chance to think about things - the same for either house - the essence of all art.

A mining town, I assume. There are slag-heaps looming up behind the houses. There are children playing on them in winter clothes. I have never been here, but I think I know what it is. I have a letter from my Grandmother's brother – at the time of her death – talking about playing games on the slag-heaps behind their house. It's a house on the main street of Egremont, Cumberland. Presumably, the house is still there. My dad was born in Canada, so he never lived there, but his mother was born there, as I said, and his older sister– my Aunt Margaret – spent her first eight years in that town and in that house. My dad took my mom to visit there when they were retired.

A crusty old fellow
he must have been.

Of course you are wondering why you are here.

None of my guests ever asks for the ride. He handles the reins quite lightly – we never seem to dip or sway. Well it isn't up to me. An outside force – of some kind or other – gets to decide. His voice is rather soothing. I break away from his eyes. I peer ahead as far as I can. Do I see a red light?

Wise men and farmers and shepherds and all.

How can I tell whether this is actually happening? I could pinch myself, but that might be true of a dream. You seem so real as I sit here beside you. Your hand was firm inside your glove. You seem as human – Santa – as anyone I know. And yet here we are on your sleigh – pulled by eight – or is it nine – tiny reindeer. Far above the ground. A slight breeze but not a strong wind. And I don't feel queasy or sense that I might fall. How do I know whether this is a dream or whether it's real?

His fire
had gone out
and he was in the dark.

A man – living and thinking.

Year after year
he was told
that Santa had refused.

They had gone out to a Christmas-tree farm. The day was clear and cold. Their four-year old son had chosen a tree that they had approved.

Scientists go by fads.

Spends the year making toys.

Helped the sick and the poor.
The Coca-Cola Company.

So the Butcher and the Baker are obviously the ones who committed the crime, said the detective's assistant.
Field and fountain, moor and mountain.
I have never willed these visits, though I enjoy them when they occur. I am alone but never lonely. I never travel with the elves. My wife remains at the pole. I love the reindeer, but we live in different realms. In the whole world, I am the only Santa Claus.

They parked the car in the parking lot. The carols were playing over the loudspeaker. Tiny snowflakes were lazily drifting down.

Settling back for a world-wide tour with Santa.
A wonderful occasion for a Santa interview.

I am interviewing Mrs. Claus! She gives me a tour of the house! A little candy-cane cottage at the North Pole! I ask a pertinent question! She doesn't know where Santa is today!

Not completely forthcoming - as we know it today - doesn't strike the eyes or the skin - something that disturbs me - the other kind of tour - think in human terms - searching for better words - we keep finding out - and on no terms - setting the agenda.

Would this be early in the century? – in the 20th Century, I mean. And is it Christmas time? – the air looks crisp and cold, though I don't feel heat or cold when I'm with you. A few wisps of snow on the cobblestones on the street. They would be celebrating Christmas at about this time. They were miners, so presents would be, I would think, quite scarce. Perhaps an orange or at least an apple in a stocking. I assume we can't go inside the house. One of my lost heritages, I guess. Neither my aunt nor my grandmother ever talked about those times.

Hold them loosely
and they might be gone.

So there really is a North Pole. I've seen it so many times on post-cards, but I've never really believed it was actually there. I guess it could serve as a hitching-post but these reindeer are all so docile that Santa would never have to tie them down. Like the horses who pulled the milk and bread wagons when I was a boy – or the horse that stopped by woods on a snowy evening. Snow is falling, just like it does at home – gently floating down to the ground. A white curtain in the sunshine on a beautiful winter day.

Bless all the dear children in thy tender care.

Santa raises a finger and points. There's a break in the curtain of snow. It's a beautiful snow-covered vision – a candy-cane house and what looks like a work-shop right beside. And elves! – a couple of elves! Two elves just opened up the work-shop door. Must be taking a break from making the children's toys. A snowball fight breaks out! More elves come out and take up sides. Too far to hear their laughter or any words. Santa sits in the sleigh and watches. He doesn't say a word. Should I ask him if I'm going to get a tour?

There was a man who thought in images. Or – perhaps he was a character, and not a man at all.

From time to time

Ten dollars dropped on the floor.
A mall-Santa who is the actual Santa Claus.
Watching Shakespeare writing a play.

a number of people

Books by Proust and James Joyce?
Books by Dickens and Lewis Carroll?
Books that tell us how we think our way through life?

have tried.

On the contrary – only an innocent person would leave a clue at the scene of a crime, said the detective. I shall arrest the Candlestick-maker for the murder of Mister Mustard in the Library because the Candle-stick-maker is the one who left no clue at the scene of the crime.

Above thy deep and dreamless sleep.

Between stops, we travel just high enough to be able to see the lights of cities, or look down on large stretches of water, between segments of land. I once had an interesting realization. We were hurtling along in a metal capsule and the pilot casually mentioned that we were flying at about a mile or two above the ground and that the temperature outside the plane was a very long way below freezing. And I realized that all of us would be dead in an instant if we suddenly found our-selves outside the plane. Similar conditions are probably what we have right here. The rules of destruction are obviously suspended as we ride along.

Chapter 3

By the way – Santa – since we're here and riding along like this – I, a simple Earthling, and you with seemingly-unlimited powers. There's a little tiny conundrum – a mystery in my family – stretching back for – I would say – about seventy years. I'm seventy-six years old, at present, as you, I assume, would know. It happened while I was seven, or eight or nine. It was when we were in the first house that my dad built, for sure.

Good tidings to you and all of your kin.

Well, my mom bought me a present. And on Christmas Day, we were all opening our presents. Socks and a sweater and always the toy that my brother and sister and I were each allowed to select from the catalogue or from a window in a store. And then – when all the presents were opened and we were cleaning up the wrapping-paper – my mom asked me, in turn, to show what I had received.

And the other

A person asking a question.
Children building a sand-castle on the beach.
A story that will probably not make a book.

flame

Do you have any proof?
A whisker, perhaps, from Santa's beard?
Something that can be matched with DNA?

was dark.

A portly white-bearded gentleman.
A long time ago, in 270 AD.
Leaves the gifts beneath the Christmas tree.

My mom had a puzzled look on her face, as I held each present up and said a few words. This is from Grandpa, and this is from Uncle Claude and on through the seven or eight presents that I had received. But the shirt! – where's the shirt? – did I forget to wrap it up? I bought a cowboy shirt that I found in just your size! Is there anything under the tree? Surely it isn't still in the cupboard! I'll go and look in just a minute! It's a beautiful shirt that I know you would love to wear!
Tobogganing down a hill.
An elf left the North Pole and started walking.

He knew who the lady was. He used to see her every Sunday. Not anymore because he went to a different church.
They built a new church in the neighbourhood. The lady stayed at the old church. So they didn't see each other anymore.

Asking Santa to solve a family mystery.
Expecting to go back into the past to sort it all out.

Sitting here with my guitar.

Strumming idly and humming a tune.
I think I'll call it a ballad.
The Ballad of Santa Claus.

I can suggest - indifferent to the agony - whatever a life-time means - don't control these things - another dimension of thought - new scientific theory - plenty of thoughts - all times are alive - hard to believe - the bottom of the ocean.

Oh! I know what place this is. This is the house where my mom spent her childhood. The Miller's House on Water Lane in Ospringe, Kent. It's only a few houses from the path that Chaucer's characters walked on their pilgrimage. My mother called it the Roman Road, but it's the London-Canterbury highway. I visited this house – when I went to England – shortly after I retired.

He carried a lantern around
in the middle of the day.

You know, I have a theory, Santa – see it as fanciful if you like – that things that go missing down here on Earth become the – 'purloined', shall we say – property of the gods. Picture Olympus as a great big supernatural 'Lost-and-Found'. So back in 1952 or 1953 or 1954 – say – when I was seven or eight or nine – there was a little boy on Olympus – perhaps the son of a lesser god – who's breast was bursting with pride as he showed the other god-children his brand-new gift from his father, when Daddy had just returned from a business-trip to Earth. A brand-new shoot-em-up, circle-the-wagons, horsey, ride-em-an-rope-em spectacular, child-human cowboy shirt.

Sipping hot chocolate from a mug.

Do you think that little god-children – stuck up there on drab Olympus – bleak winds and swirling mists – would like to be able to live like us – with all the commercial toys and sugary candy that are – presumably – forbidden up there to the children of the gods? And are there gods who cheat a bit – bring back contraband from their trips – when they are sent to stir up mischief or soothe the troubled waters down here on the earth? I have a box that my father made – it has all my souvenirs – hockey cards and cub-scout badges and a certificate of proficiency or two. Maybe some sage and solemn Olympian has a similar box – made of marble – in which he keeps a worn-out, childhood, Earthling cowboy shirt. Yours – Santa – is the eye that can tell me – after all these years of wondering – if this is true.

The explorer
was startled
by a huge red glow.

A character – living and thinking.

Krampus was told
that Santa
would not even send a representative.

A few more trimmings for the tree. It was in the livingroom. Some decorations from the past and some brand-new.

Christmas Eve was relaxing and cheerful. All the presents were wrapped and hid. They would bring them out when the kids were safely in bed.

Or to be kinder, let us say that scientists go through changes-of-theory.

The help of his elves.
A monk named St. Nicholas.
Born to a wealthy family.

So my question for you, Santa – since you have extra-sensory powers. Cast your mind back seventy years – picture the scene of my mom in the store – driving home and unpacking her things – putting the presents away in the cupboard – wrapping the presents on the bed – putting the presents under the tree, and then Christmas Day and all of us checking under the tree and in the cupboard in my parents' bedroom. Zero in on the moment of loss, please, and tell me – after all these years – seventy years of mystery and speculation – what in the world ever became of my cowboy shirt?
Skating for miles on a pond.
It's reassuring to know that I can walk in any direction and still get where I am going, thought the elf.

Last-minute shoppers crowded the aisles. He always enjoyed the last-minute crowds. It reminded him of Christmas when he was a boy.

His wife was the Christmas-shopper. She bought presents in both their names. All he had to do was to buy some presents for her.

Offering Santa one of my interesting theories.
Hoping he'll be impressed by the logic that I apply.

When was Santa born?

Or was he created?
Guess I'll have to check the facts.
For sure I'll call it The Ballad of Santa Claus.

Living in every moment - santa taking a break - how real they seem to be - only seem that way - how many thoughts - the idea-structure - only one santa - if i had an idea - locked in a routine - whatever occurs to you.

I'm sure we can't go in, but I've already been inside. My son, Craig, and I visited Faversham. We stayed in a pub in the market town. And we walked out here, to Ospringe, with a lady named Pam, and stood on this street – Water Lane – and looked at this house – the Miller's House, where my mom spent her childhood years. Oh she would talk about their lives, how they toasted the bread on forks over the fire, after dipping it into the fat left over from the roast. And how their grandad used to take them out for walks. There were six of them in all – her dad was a Royal Marine, so he wasn't always home at Christmas time. And a lady came out to the street, and invited us in for tea. And I sat in the house and sipped my tea and chatted about how my ancestors used to live here, years ago. And when I climbed the stairs to look at the bedrooms, I burst into tears. My mom had told me that she used to take a candle – at bedtime – and she and the other kids would climb those stairs. My mom was dead by that time – all of her family used to live here. I had missed seeing them – and talking with them – by eighty years.

Baba Yaga
is on the prowl.

A dry and desiccated desert. Santa comes in for a landing on a bank of sand. I don't feel any heat at all. We're protected from the heat. We were in Vegas once and the thermometer showed one hundred and seventeen degrees. Can't tell where this desert is – Santa doesn't seem inclined to say. Obviously the reindeer don't feel the ferocity of the sun at all. They seem to know what Santa wants. They just stand and await their cue. Let Santa sit and think and then move on.

Mittens pinned to a snowsuit.

Burnt and parched and dried to a frazzle. I assume this desert used to be the bed of an ancient lake. Flat as a pancake – layers of sediment from thousands – maybe millions – of years. A couple of buzzards off in the distance. Tightening the circles above their next meal. I've heard they can sense when you're getting close the end of your trail. How can anything bloom in these conditions? Wonder if Santa is wondering the same? How many days does he spend in these places – just sitting and watching and thinking his private thoughts? Or is the agenda being tailored specifically for me?

The man was thought by others to be a jolly, rather uncomplicated old elf. But the man – the character – the elf – was deeply troubled.

Pilgrims

A tangle of boots at the kitchen door.
Kids skating on a rink long after dark.
Watching the baby Jesus being born.

have trekked

Didn't know about the Krampus?

Never heard of it before?

Surely somewhere in your mind these images have lurked?

on religious journeys.

Flying along beside Santa. I grip the side of the seat but I don't feel uneasy at all. He's an old master at the handling of a team of tiny, flying reindeer. This trip reminds me of taking a ship along the north shore of the Mediterranean. I wanted to see Gibraltar, as my grandfather had served there as a Royal Marine. And I knew that we would pass it – in the dark – about two a.m. And so I was on the lookout, as we passed along the land – and strings of lights along the shore would disappear in the blackness and then a new string of lights would appear. I had no idea what island or what country I was seeing – all I knew was that Gibraltar would be two o'clock. Here, I have no idea where we're going in the dark.

A scarf that hides the whole face.

I have heard rumours of a land with no ice and no snow.

Chapter 4

Everything seems to be working in harmony. Santa and the team of tiny reindeer – plunging through the night with me aboard. I ease back in the seat a bit and wait for Santa's answer, but he doesn't seem too eager to respond. So – you mentioned, Santa, that you have had other – visitors – before. Can I ask who some of these people might have been? Do you do this very often – play host to people from daily-life down below? Give them a tour of the places that you are showing me? There's all kinds of questions I'd like to ask you. I might want to write a book about you some day.

Peace on the earth, good will to men.

How can I put this, John? You are overstepping your bounds, as an inquisitor. Of course, you couldn't know the rules of this mythical realm. I can tell you certain things – other things are not to be of your purview. No one tells me this – I somehow simply know.

The two flames

A person explaining a set of rules.
A photo of a boy in a cowboy shirt.
Reindeer grazing in a grassy field.

pawed at each other

So you fancy yourself as a writer?
Always at work on a current book?
Always searching for a way to express yourself?

like two kittens in a basket.

Slides down the chimney.
Gave away all that he had.
Dressed in a red suit with a black belt.

It is obvious that God created the Big Bang, said the minister.

Mighty dread had seized their troubled mind.

But what I can tell you, continues Santa, is that there are some people on Earth – some of the people that you rub elbows with in your daily rounds – perhaps some people you actually know – who have known Santa Claus, in the same way that you are coming to know me now. Who have spent a day or a moment – it is a different measurement of time – here, in my sleigh – with my reindeer and me. And yes – since you are wondering – there are nine.

She looked at him as she waited for her tea. She didn't know who he was. But the boy knew something about the lady.

The lady was his Godmother. She didn't know him anymore. To her, he was just a little boy.

Finding that Santa is not completely forthcoming.

His comments imply a degree of image-restraint.

I am opening my closet! There are a dozen costumes inside! I have a choice of costumes! I have collected them over time! I am wondering which costume I should wear!

A soul-cleansing talk - a series of images - children will be asleep - basic dynamic of life - proposing that we consolidate - a trifle convoluted - seem so real - even that is ambivalent - anywhere in the here and now - carnage on a massive scale.

Well this is my boyhood home. On Oak Street, St. Thomas, Ontario. There are two family houses, of course. My father built them both by hand. One is still standing and one has been torn down. I set my novel – *Pinafore Park* – in the first house that Dad built, though the incident that the novel is based on happened years before he built it. The two houses were only a field away from each other. My family didn't change when we made the move. My Christmas memories are the same for either house.

He would light it
in the agora at noon.

And yes, the nose is certainly red, as you can see by the ruddy glow. That was a foggy night, as you know from the song, when the full force of Rudolph's nose was a blessing to me. Most Christmas Eves are quite routine – that was a very rare affair. Since that time, he has had the lead – each Christmas – of my sleigh.

O sing of fragrant flowers' breath.

I am, John, what you would probably call 'a fictional character', but I see myself as nonetheless real for that. I only know what I know. I don't know God personally. I have certain powers and yet I am limited in the things that I can do. I can't stop wars, for instance, or heal broken hearts or feed the hungry. I can deliver toys and – and this is what people don't seem to realize about me – I can suggest that people give gifts to others as well.

He edged
ever closer
to the rim of the valley.

An entity – living and thinking.

And on no terms
would Santa
attend himself.

They had a fireplace in their home. No fire on Christmas Eve. Clean the ashes out so Santa can come right down.

Their oldest son was four. He asked a lot of questions. Other things he knew and would gladly tell.

Once it was thought that a scientist could conduct a pure experiment.

Popular Santa Claus advertisements.
Travelled the countryside.
Refreshes himself with milk and cookies.

It is obvious that the Big Bang created God, said the scientist.
Now ye need not fear the grave.

I can visit what you call 'the past'– in a sense – but I can't change it. You would probably call it 're-visiting', but that's not the right term for me. All times are alive for me at the very same time. I am living in every moment when I visit what you call 'the past'. I am living my life at that moment for the very first time. So – as for your cowboy shirt – I cannot go back in time. I have no idea where it is – where your mother put it that day. I cannot go back and help her to find it now.

Buying presents for just one person. What a relaxing way to shop. The last few years he had taken his oldest son.

There had already been a visit with Santa Claus. The whole family had gone along. He and his wife, their four-year-old son and their brand-new baby boy.

Wondering why I am thinking of my ancestral families.

Wondering if Santa is the one who is guiding my thoughts.

I interview some of the elves! They show me through the workshop! A tiny building holding a multitude of toys! I ask a pertinent question! They don't know where Santa is today!

The reason-for-being - a whim on my part - many struggle to survive - will be shaped by - but then, the complications - might be true of a dream - live in different realms - just be riding on the airways - kilometers or miles - where i would choose to go.

All of us gathered around the table. A table my

dad had made. A great big turkey on a platter. Bowls of steaming potatoes and corn. Beans and ham and dressing. A great big pitcher of gravy too. And all of us bowing our heads and saying our prayer. 'For what we are about to receive, may we be truly thankful.' My mom, my dad, my brother and my sister. My Uncle Ken and my Aunt Margaret and my Uncle Claude. My dad's mother while she was alive. She died when I was nine. By this time, of course, my mom's mom was dead too. My Grandfather – Walter Davies – lighting a flame on the Christmas cake. He would pour the brandy out and strike a match. A dish of ice-cream along with the Christmas cake, and then we would all open our presents in the living room.

Follows Santa
without him knowing.

Penguins! Thousands of penguins! Obviously this is the southernmost pole. I don't see a pole anywhere but it has to be here. I've seen penguins at the zoo. And in those documentaries they show. It's really astounding how they divide the parental roles. One will watch the germinating egg – huddle above it to keep it warm – and the other will slide down an icy slope and plunge into the waves. Water that's cold enough to freeze but never freezes. Swallowing fish to come back and regurgitate for its spouse. Then they switch on the egg and the other one takes a turn.

Yet in thy dark streets shineth.

They used to have penguins in Newfoundland. I read about it in Farley Mowat's book. My mom got it from the Book-of-the-Month Club when I lived at home. The early explorers would take a board and set it between the rocks and the gunwales. Then the New-foundland-penguins would walk right up the plank. Then all that was needed was a sturdy club. Bash in the head as each one arrived. They'd keep waddling up the gang-plank. One after another, like cattle or sheep. 'Til you had enough meat to salt away in the hold. Wonder whether Santa knows all this? Wonder if he's ever going to talk? Wonder if my voice would make any sound if I spoke to him?

He was locked in a routine which was one of great joy to him, in enhancing the enjoyment of others, but he could not remain unaware of the realities that he saw all around him. His own response to those realities was positive, but narrow in the extreme.

Pirates

A house in a wood-lot near a village.
The spaces between the mountains in a range.
A person who uses logic to figure things out.

have sailed

Books of plays, poems, novels?
Every genre that writers have made?
Working hard at designing a genre of your own?

in search of spoil.

It is obvious that nothing was created, said the man who was an atheist and a nihilist.
And of the news that came to them.
It's quite interesting to watch the reindeer as they

fly. They act like real reindeer in many ways. The breeze blows through their fur – the wind pins back their ears – their muscles move as their feet move through the air. But the temperature up here doesn't affect them – as it doesn't affect me. And they don't pant as I understand reindeer would do. And they don't seem to know exhaustion. That's how wolves tire them out to bring them down.

Chapter 5

Riding along beside Santa in the sleigh. Below us the lights twinkle in the dark. I have no idea where we're going – and Santa doesn't seem inclined to act as my guide. The reindeer seem to have a sense of purpose – enough to keep them in the air without any wings. Well – so much for the missing cowboy shirt. I had hoped that 'Santa's Search for the Missing McGuffin' would yield enough of a plot to make a heart-warming, charming little book. Now – what else might make a good story? I venture to ask a question that I am dying to ask. Do you know such – well, celebrities – as the Easter Bunny? Do you all get together, perhaps, once in a while? Are there red-carpet gatherings in the supernatural life? Do you swap stories of how it is to be iconic figures? Or do you all operate – travel – on your own separate paths?

Breath making a cloud in the cold air.

I know about him, John – what he is and what he does and what he stands for. But I probably don't know any more about him than you. I can speculate as to what it is like to be the Easter Bunny, simply by considering how alike we seem to be. But we exist in different zones – different dimensions. I have never bumped into the Easter Bunny on my travels and don't expect to – nor the Tooth Fairy, nor Jack Frost, nor any of those. It's not like the gods, all living together on Mount Olympus – interacting and interfering in each other's lives. Each of us has our separate existence and our separate role.

Placing the eyes on a snowman.

It's a little hard to swallow what Santa is telling me. That he doesn't know God personally makes sense to me, given the limits on his powers. That he doesn't know the Easter Bunny is harder to accept, but I'll take his word. But – that he doesn't know Jack Frost is un-believable. If I were dreaming up his answers, I would have the two of them be the best of friends. How could they live at the same latitude for what might be eons and never come across each other at all? I should ask him about Frosty the Snowman just to see what he'll say.

The two flames

Holding out a handful of oats.
The Miller's House on Water Lane.
An elf busily working at the South Pole.

hissed at each other

So what is the point of fiction?
Just an academic guessing-game?
Trying to guess what the writer is trying to say?

like two snakes in a nest.

Also called Nicholas of Bari.
Receives letters from children.
Images drawn by cartoonist Thomas Nast.

Oh I know what you'll ask me next. Do I know the Olympic gods? Do I know the Norse gods and all the ancient ones? Well, I am ancient too, you know, at least as a force in life – I didn't always have the external appearance that I do now – but I have never come into contact with any other ancient ones in my many thousands of years. I know them as you would know them – and nothing more. We all interact with humans – or so I read in the books – but we never interact with each other at all. Have I known Cleopatra? – Shakespeare? – and so many other illustrious ones? Did I deliver – or suggest – a gift for them in their day? Yes, of course I did – using your choice of terms. The point I would make is that I am visiting them now. If I am timeless – as I am – then there is no past and no future for me. Either there is nothing – a blank – a void – or there is the present – the continuous-present – all the time. Cleopatra is always the Queen – Shakespeare is always writing his plays – Jesus is always a little babe in his mother's arms.

A turkey sizzling in the oven.

A school bus full of children stopped in front of Santa's workshop.

He stood and watched the lady. She put the milk and sugar into her tea. Suddenly something fluttered to the floor.

He knelt and picked it up. It was a ten-dollar bill. It had fallen when the lady turned away.

So happy to get a peek behind the veil.
Asking Santa how the immortals interact.

Have to look up Santa's origins.

Does Christmas pre-date the birth of Christ?
Must be plenty of facts I can process
For my Ballad of Santa Claus.

Watch the germinating egg - not deviating at all - nothing was created - it is obvious - the power of images - alone but never lonely - do the dogged research - convincing myself - a million ways to think - a way of breaking away.

Well Barbados! Of course! A little hotel with a pool and access to the beach. We were two young working-class kids whose families had never travelled anywhere, and here we were with two professional salaries — two teachers getting paid a good day's pay. So we booked a flight and spent Christmas in Barbados. Sun and sand and warm water in December. A dream vacation in every Canadian mind. Sunset Crest Villas — that's the very room where we stayed. That balcony with the same soak-up-the sun easy-chairs. Moonlight shimmering on the water. Palm trees swaying in the breeze. A sip or two of rum in the shade of the sail.

Trying to stay light
in a world which he saw as very dark.

But what about the decades? What about the passage of time? Cleopatra lost her throne — Shakespeare grew ill and died — Jesus was crucified and rose again and went up to heaven to sit at the right hand of God. Well — all of that is continually happening. You are seventy-six years old — you tell me so as you sit beside me, here, on my sleigh. But you are also nine years old — and I am visiting you this Christmas. And you are nineteen, and twenty-nine, and thirty-nine and on and on – all on what you would think of as the very same day. I don't exist out of time – I exist in time, but independently of time. There's a difference in those concepts, I'm sure you'll agree.

Saying grace with our heads bowed.

Now – dare you ask if you will be ever be ninety-nine? Well the future is still to come. It is the thing that I cannot know. I live in all moments from now back to the beginning of time. But I have no crystal ball. I can't tell how long you will live. All I know is that if you live, I will know. And I will visit you when you are ninety-nine. And either bring you something that suits you or put a little thought in someone's head – someone who loves you and wants the best for you. If you are there, I will let you see me. We can continue our talk of today. We'll probably both have thought of a lot more things to say – with a lot more conundrums that we can discuss but never solve.

Shovelling the sidewalk.

Sorry I don't have what you would call 'wisdom'. I have no idea why there are continuous wars. I don't know why people die early. Why some spend their lives in pain. All I know is that other people can, if they wish, make their own and other's lives a little less painful – reduce the quotient of the agony that drives so many people insane. I have been here since the beginning of time. I am the spirit of all things positive in the world.

The explorer was amazed
at what he saw
below.

This is the essence of all art.

In fact,
there's never been a meeting
in all these years.

Their younger boy was just a baby. He didn't have any questions to ask. Everything about Christmas was fine with him.

Last minute preparations for Santa. Their four-year-old knew exactly what to set out. Amazing that he knew what Santa and Rudolph would need.

A pure experiment – by definition – is an experiment in which the subject is observed without any interaction – any influence – any distortion – being presented or incurred by either the scientist or the subject of the exercise.

White fur trim, black boots, and a soft red cap.
Known to be kind to children.
Born in the village of Patara.

Gifts are a way of making human contact. Giving something that you value personally to someone else. You know – the ultimate gift is the gift of the essence of the self. Sometimes it's treasured – sometimes it's not. Sometimes even the gift of a heart is left out in the rain. I have no control over the value that is placed on each gift by the recipient – I do have influence over the heart of the one who gives. Give with love and hope to be given love in return.

A car getting stuck in the snow.

It was summer, so there was no ice or snow on the northern roads.

They had sat on Santa's knees. Their mom had dressed them in matching sweaters. They had their picture taken in a mall.

He had told Santa what he wanted. He had asked Santa for a train. So they wouldn't take time to seek out Santa Claus.

Wondering why we are visiting such extreme locations.

Wondering if Santa is the one who is guiding my thoughts.

Wondering whether Santa is setting the agenda or am I.

I had never heard of Krampus.
At least I didn't know the name.
I wonder if Krampus should figure
In my Ballad of Santa Claus?

Might not be a dream - by what or by whom - checking everyone's i.d. - the reindeer teeth - only know what i know - show what i had received - they re-created themselves - a wonderland of white - snow-covered vision - myths have murky origins.

But Barbados wasn't Canada. No skating on the rink. No shovelling the walk of snow. Christmas carols over the radio, yes, and white spray on store windows by painters who had never seen actual snow. Christmas dinner in a restaurant. No Christmas tree on our balcony or in our room. And most of all, no family for my wife or for me. The year before we had two Christmases — one with her family and one with mine. That Christmas we thought of home as we lay on the beach. It was Christmas to the Barbadians, but it wasn't Christmas to us. It was the first – and last – Christmas we didn't spend at home.

Steals the toys
that Santa leaves behind.

This is really something. I've never seen the bottom of the ocean. All these fish are so brightly-coloured. There's what looks like an eighteenth-century wreck. Spars and yard-arms and even the wheel where the captain used to stand. Here's a whale opening wide and scooping a whole school of frantic victims. Keeping my eye out for sharks, but Santa doesn't seem to be worried at all. Eight tiny reindeer and Rudolph would make a delectable feast. We're not getting wet, so we're obviously in a sea-proof bubble of some kind. We're probably invisible to everything in the ocean but ourselves. The reindeer stand and wait as if they're still on land. There's not much chance that any of us will drown.

Hanging Christmas stockings on the mantle.

This is obviously one of the trenches. Santa hasn't said a word. He just took the reins and off we went again. Plunging down and down and down and down and down. Let's see – there's the Marianas Trench and then there's the – um – the Mid-Atlantic Trench? – or am I thinking of the Mid-Atlantic Ridge? I wonder if Santa knew about these under-ocean landmarks before they were found. The air bubbles out of the fissures. It's supposed to be hundreds – or thousands – of degrees. I'd be boiling to death if Santa wasn't around. Nothing to do but to sit here and think, I guess. No point in trying to leave the sleigh. Santa hasn't said a word in all this time. He sits and thinks beside me. I sit and think beside him. I wonder if my words would bubble if I asked him why we are here?

One day, he was surprised to see a certain person in his sleigh. It was one whose sensibility he knew.

There is nothing

A group of people swapping stories.
Watching the news on TV.
A visit to the core of the earth.

that is new

The clash of 'mighty opposites'?
Battles of minds as much as of swords?
Images hoping that you will lead them into the fray?

in the heavens.

Einstein started with a simple question. Why does a cup of tea – travelling at sixty miles per hour – not blow back in your face? The shallow answer was that the tea was inside a train. The deeper question was why the tea did not blow back in your face – when you were holding the cup of tea – and you were going sixty miles an hour too. So where am I at the moment – as I sit beside Santa Claus – relative to both space and time?
We all know that Santa's coming.
They were surprised to find a pad-lock on the door.

Chapter 6

You see, John, I have, as I mentioned, certain powers – what you would call 'magical powers' – but I don't have the ability to go back in time. So I can't take you back – or even go back alone – and pinpoint the minute when your mom lost the cowboy shirt. And – if you think about it – the shirt would not still be a shirt when we – or I alone – would try to bring it back to the present time. And besides – it doesn't strike me that it would still be able to fit.

Hark! The herald angels sing.

Oh I've had lots of requests, of course, from others who've come along – people who've suddenly turned up on my sleigh. They want to see the Big Bang – or see Shakespeare writing a play – or, of course, see the baby Jesus being born – but – and I'm always sorry to disappoint them – but I just have to tell them – bluntly – that time is not a door, with a room behind it that I can take them to.

The two flames

An item of clothing that no longer fits.
A group of animals listening to a talk.
A series of images as visual as a dream.

grew large

Are you making fun of Santa?
Is that what this is about?
Don't you appreciate his contribution to human-kind?

as the world grew large.

A Bishop at an early age.
Born in the fourth century.
The poem 'Twas the Night Before Christmas.

Many eons ago, the people of the earth decided that their planet was no longer habitable.
Years ago, on a deep winter night.
But I can take them anywhere – anywhere in the here and now. And – just in case you're wondering – I don't always go to the places where I'm taking you, John. A while ago, a load of kids appeared in my sleigh. So I played the jolly host. I took them to many different places on the earth – let them see other kids in the other cities and other fields and villages at play.

The lady was walking away. She was carefully balancing the cup of tea. He walked after her, holding the ten-dollar bill.
"Excuse me," he said. She was sitting on the aisle. She was balancing the tea-cup on her knee.

Finding Santa's logic a trifle convoluted.
Can he go back into the past or can he not?

There's someone sitting at my computer! The head

is slumped against the screen! I have the urge to write a novel! I won't be able to use my computer – unless I open the head of this person and wriggle inside!

Works on many levels - a break in the curtain - an interesting realization - to sort it all out - don't see any end - looking him in the eye - anything under the tree - wait patiently in harness - thinking of all the topics - all that was needed.

The little house on Harmony Road, in Ancaster, Ontario. Just my wife and I at first. Then the three boys came along. Many memories cling to that house. My wife would decorate every corner – every nook and niche and mantel – with decorations of Christmas and winter and family things. We had a fireplace in the living room, but no fires on the night when Santa would arrive.

Ded Moroz
was deeply troubled.

I took them to various happy places around the globe. Of course, I don't exist in time – I mean I don't think in minutes and hours – so I never know when they've had a long day – or when a trip seems that it's about to come to an end. We'll just be riding on the airways – chatting about all the places we've been – or of where they would like to go – and then – suddenly – I'll be sitting here all alone in my sleigh.

Sealed in the stone-cold tomb.

Now – earlier on, you asked a question. Something like – how often does this happen? How often do I take people for rides in my sleigh? Well, as I've said, I don't think in human terms. Once a year? – once a day? I have no idea. I have memories – but they aren't arranged in time. Your mom and dad, for instance – I would know them if they were here, but I can't go back in time – in the way that you understand that concept – and see them as people who are no longer – now – alive.

A group of animals
was sitting
in a circle.

A man – responding to his life-experience and thinking.

"But Santa and I
are in the same business,"
explained the Krampus.

A glass of milk for Santa. And a carrot for Rudolph. Right here on the kitchen table.

It had been a difficult evening. Whether to drink the glass of milk? Whether to bite the carrot or not? Either way he was in the position of offering 'truth'.

But then the scientists' wind-sock changed direction.

One of the most popular minor saints.
Used his fortune to help others.
Harper's Weekly, beginning in 1863.

So they established a colony on the moon and moved all the people of the earth to live on the moon. *On a cold winter's night that was so deep.*

I don't control these things – I don't make any of the rules. A myth has been created – I don't know by what or by whom – by Charles Dickens, if you like, or Clement Moore – and I have all the freedoms and all of the restraints that come along with that mythical enterprise. The only king and the only peasant in my realm.

So they headed for the ladies' department. Searching for presents to buy for Mom. They rounded a corner of a display and suddenly stopped.

It was Santa! It was Santa, as sure as sure! Santa-coat and boots and gloves and hat and beard!

Convincing myself that these are actual reindeer.

After all, they drink real water and graze on real grass.

I am riding in a sleigh! It is pulled by eight tiny reindeer! Led by a reindeer with a shiny red nose! We fly above the rooftops! Beside me, holding the reins, is an interesting entity!

Worlds in tension - rubbish heaps are filled - nothing more creative - similar conditions - hasn't been driving itself - it was a mystery - his brand-new gift - doesn't affect them - years of mystery and doubt - lives in a different sphere.

Mostly memories of our oldest boy in the little house in Ancaster. He was five when we made the move to Cayuga. The other two boys were three and just-arrived. We'd go out to a farm and buy a Christmas tree – put it up in the living room. Have our own little Christmas on Christmas morning and then the whole little house would be full on Christmas afternoon. All the Passfields and the Murrays under one roof. That was the house of the reindeer-teeth. And the house of the boy-Santa hidden under the snow-white beard. And we'd go to the church for the service on Christmas Eve. And Christmas was always white – always plenty of snow in those days. Always shovelling and great-big snow-tires on the car. A wonderland of white – or does it only seem that way? Christmas Days on Harmony Road were the same as a dream.

> *It was the sword*
> *of the Unconquered Sun.*

We are on the side of a mountain. Santa waves his gloved hand and the reindeer are unhitched and un-harnessed from the sleigh. They sniff the air and take short tentative steps into the flowing mountain stream. The sun shines on the glacier far above us. The grass is green and wavy here and no doubt lush for a reindeer to eat. They look like actual reindeer, of course, but do they actually need food and drink? I wonder if these reindeer are actually real?

The silent stars go by.

Another wave of Santa's gloved hand and the rein-deer are hitched and harnessed. I wait for a wave of the hand, but I am expected, I see, to climb, on my own, back into the sleigh. Santa is quite a robust fellow, but he bounds back onto the seat. He clucks his voice and flips the reins and we rise up and float in the sky. We ne-gotiate the spaces between the mountains in the range. Have these visits all been symbolic, perhaps? What are these mountains, I wonder, supposed to mean to me?

But the man – the character – the elf – did not articulate his feelings. He did not articulate his thoughts.

There is nothing

Wondering whether it's kilometers or miles.
A fictional character who sees himself as real.
Three little boys in matching sweaters.

that is new

Achilles and Hector?
Macduff and Macbeth?
Are Santa and the Krampus not a natural for you?

in the waves.

As time went by, the people of the moon found it logical to believe that the earth was made of green cheese.

A snow plough filling in the driveway.

That mountain stop was the first place-stop for Santa that I would say approaches what I would call 'normal'. The reindeer acted like actual reindeer would. Wonder where he'll take me now? So far, it's all been houses and rooms. Wonder when we'll start to see people. Maybe the scenes of my early childhood. Something like Dickens, but without the need for the guilt, the remorse, and the change of heart.

Chapter 7

This is quite an opportunity for me, Santa, because – you see – I'm interested in the concept of myth. Myth – it seems to me – is the basis of all literature. And it's the basis of all literature because it's the basic dynamic of life. We human beings take our experience – our own and that of others – of an individual, a group or a whole society – and turn it into imagery – significant imagery – which we place in patterns of potential-meaning – and when the image-patterns are interpreted, we have a myth. Now myths are highly contentious – for an individual and for a tribe – so all of life – and therefore all of literature – is the battle of the myths. The Othello-myth, the Desdemona-myth, the Iago-myth. The cultural-myth: the myth of Santa – the author-myth: the myth of Shakespeare – do you see? And then there's the myth – the reader-comprehension-myth – that is created in the reader's mind, as these literary-images take their place in the folds of the grey-matter and have their say. So Santa, you are a mythical creature – as much as any of the characters from the greatest books of all time. That's why it's a privilege to get to talk with you this way.

Putting another log on the fire.

Well, I am a mythical creature, John. There's no doubt in my mind about that. But you realize that I know little about how it's done. Clement Moore wrote the poem – about the eight tiny reindeer and the sleigh. Until he did, I had only myself for getting around. And then the fellow wrote the song and there was Rudolph – Johnny Marks from a poem by Robert May. But even if I had thought of Rudolph, John, I couldn't have altered the myth. I am a myth – you are a human. Humans make myths – myths are made. I am as malleable as clay, John – you are the potter and I am the vase. I am the work of art and you are the artisan.

Each flame would coil and cling

A recipe for a literary concept.
Children playing on the slag-heaps.
Characters who are real and who are not.

to as much as it could

Always thinking that books are like life?
Always thinking that life is like books?
How we think in ink and paper and in our heads?

of the globe.

Published in 1823.
Orphaned as a teen.
Loads his sleigh with toys.

But suppose you make me the Christmas Bunny? Or give me a dog-cart pulled by mice? Or have me ride through the air on a sleigh with a team of eight tiny unicorns? – or unicorns the size of Percherons? Well, many myths are given birth, John – many struggle to survive. The rubbish heaps are filled with myths that did not take hold. A myth – to have any force – must be believed. The eight tiny reindeer – the bright red nose – you'd be hard-pressed, now, to set these images aside. But if the unicorn-story gains traction – then that's how I'll get around next Christmas Eve. Myth is a constantly-changing container of shaped-belief. It is constantly being built-up and being torn-down.

Is a fairy tale they say.

By error an elf was created at the South Pole.

"This dropped on the floor. It fell out of your purse. I picked it up off the floor."

What if she didn't believe him? She sat there balancing her teacup. She was looking him in the eye.

All he could do was tell her. He held the ten-dollar bill in his hand. "It fell on the floor when you bought your cup of tea."

Wondering whether Santa knows how ideas are processed.

Wondering whether Santa knows of the battles that are being fought.

Was Santa born?
Or was he created?
That should be the opening verse
In my Ballad of Santa Claus.

Didn't have any questions - thinking of all the topics - sage and solemn olympian - assume you are very familiar - dare you ask - wrapped and hid - logical to believe - the one i decided to do - not as cosy as I thought - allowed to enter the hall.

Well this is where we live now. Our home for forty-one years. Bought a wood-lot and had a house built years ago. Our three boys grew up in this house. Now our grandchildren come to visit. Rural Route 5, Cayuga, Ontario. Too many memories to count. Many stages over the years. Many people have been in this house – at Christmas time and all year – who are not alive now.

It had snowed
the night before.

New elves are being created, John, you know. We need more elves every year. As the population grows, we need more helpers in Santa's workshop. Of course, we don't make a toy for every child, as you can imagine – we're supernatural, but not god-powered, you know – but we do need seeds to enable the toys to grow. The loaves-and-fishes story, you realize, started with actual loaves and actual fishes. But there's something even I don't understand. Elves are created – they are wonderful – they don't die. Fine. But some are created as teen-aged elves – and some are created as middle-aged elves – and some are created even older than you or I.

Stacking the firewood in the shed.

You know, I don't know whether it has actually occurred to you, John, but sometimes one of those Santas in all those malls is actually me. Oh I know people joke about pulling Santa's beard, and occasionally a mischievous boy will do so, and it can be rather painful when it happens. But, of course, the presence of a real beard isn't incontrovertible proof that the person with the real beard is actually me. Take a close look at some of those old pictures you have in your drawer – or in your computer-file. Perhaps this is the lap that you – or perhaps your sons – were sitting on when you were all just boys.

An elephant,
a giraffe,
a wildebeest.

A character – responding to his life-experience and thinking.

"We both
keep watch
over the boys and girls.

Early to rise and down to the kitchen. Four-year old fingers tickling his feet. "I wonder if he did?"

There was the proof! – the hair stood on end! The glass of milk had all been swallowed! – the carrot had been chewed! – by reindeer-teeth! Santa and Rudolph had come to visit, as sure as sure!

The power that adults have over children. The malleability of a young child's mind. The responsibility of being an adult in what is essentially a child's world.

He felt odd all Christmas Day. The presents were opened. The two boys played with their brand-new toys.

A new concept – a new theory – came into being.

Stops at each child's house.
A secret gift-giver.
Wore the traditional red Bishop robes.

But – I shouldn't be surprised that an elf can never

have a childhood, John – as neither did I. I was created – not born at all. No mother, no father, no childhood or youth. I was created at the age that I seem to be now. Well – it's not to be regretted. I accept my lot in life. I think about it only when I spend time with someone like you.

And in case you didn't hear.

He immediately set up shop and began to make toys.

Santa seemed to be taking a break. He held a sandwich in his hand. The sandwich fit right through the beard and into his mouth.

The four-year-old hand tightened on his! The four-year-old stood there paralyzed! Santa saw them and turned and spoke to the four-year-old boy!

Wondering why Santa doesn't provide any commentary.

He's as mysterious as the horse to Robert Frost.

Was Santa twinned with another creature?
Do they grapple all over the world?
Should these two be the 'mighty opposites'
In my Ballad of Santa Claus?

Just a handle - even i don't understand - the unconquered sun - children on the beach - we can't go in - knowing in a twinkle - what santa would need - still be able to fit - this new variant - protected from the heat.

We had a pond – which we still have – and we would skate out there for hours. The kids would all bring friends and play and never seem to get tired. Hot chocolate while I blew the snow off the rink. I rigged up lights so the kids could play out there in the dark. And we always heated with wood, so there was plenty of wood to stack. I had a tractor and a chainsaw and a trailer. And we would all pitch in and stack the wood in the cellar. And then rub our hands as the kindling blazed in the stove. And Christmases were bountiful. My wife would prepare for days. She would decorate the house – still does – with all the artwork that the kids had made in school over the years. And the table would groan with plenty – help yourself and take a seat. When everyone was seated we'd say a prayer – 'for what we are about to receive, may we be truly thankful'. Then we'd all dig in and eat our Christmas feast. Thirty people in this house. Old slides of Christmases gone by. All the Christmases that are pleasant memories now. Our house won't be full in a couple of days – Covid will see to that – but our kids and grand-kids are planning to make it home. Things are getting bad again – new restrictions for travel and distancing and masks are being recommended on every newscast. Just my wife and I if Covid gets much worse.

He raised it over
his defenseless opponent.

The sleigh comes to a stop. Santa slackens the reins. We are at the core of the earth – I'm sure we are. I can't think of anywhere else that we could be. Massive movements of what I assume to be molten rock – flowing forward and ebbing back. This is obviously magma. If there was air down here, there would surely be plenty of flame. I don't feel any heat, though I'm sure it's producing thousands of thermal degrees. Santa sits and watches the magma. The colours are bright and clean and clear. They say that they colour the photos from outer-space, but we are actually here, below the earth's crust. I assume that these colours are what our eyes can actually see. The magma flows in an endless mass as we sit and watch like tourists on a bus. The reindeer shake their shoulders and quietly stamp their feet. They seem to be waiting for us to move on. They don't seem to be all that interested in what we can see.

Carving the slices of turkey.

It's amazing to be down here – sitting in a sleigh beneath the crust of the earth's surface. I can actually see two layers of rock – two tectonic plates. I know they don't move this quickly. They're massive in the extreme, but they're moving at a pace that I can see. I can see them moving towards each other – touching – scraping – grinding away. Each one sees itself as an implacable force – like two stags – or a couple of rams. Something is going to have to give somewhere up above. There could be a giant tsunami – or a massive earthquake could occur. People will pay the price of what is happening down here, under the ground. I look at Santa. He is looking at the plates as they grind with such massive force. He doesn't say a word or look at me.

He communicated in images. He took the guest to all the places that expressed his thoughts and feelings in image-terms.

There is nothing

A detective who reads the absence of a clue.
Two people who go to a different church.

Colouring the pictures in Sunday School.

that is new

A writer lives through a book?
Learning how to write a book?
And this become the book that we have just read?

in the soil.

I don't know why Santa is taking me to all these places. He hasn't said a word all the time we've been here. And I haven't said a word to him – not a word – though I've had a few interesting thoughts. Something tells me not to say anything. I have the feeling that if I speak, I won't be heard.

Wiping the frost from a window.

By Christmas, he plans to deliver presents all over the world.

Chapter 8

A nagging sense of suspicion has been curdling my thoughts as Santa and I have been flying and chatting away. A little logic might serve to wave these doubts aside. So – is Santa actually telling me anything that I don't already know? Perhaps it's ninety percent of what I already know and ten percent of what I hadn't known until now. If so, that would prove, I'm sure, that this is not a dream. Because if this is a dream, then Santa couldn't possibly tell me anything that I don't already know. Or could he? Or – could it be that what's new to me is a case of my creative imagination? Perhaps I'm standing on rock but imagining life in the clouds.

High in the heavens a star shone bright.

I look sideways at Santa from time to time. If he is aware of my scrutiny, he doesn't let on. No – he doesn't look back at me. But I'm wondering – deeply wondering, just the same – is the Santa who sits beside me in this sleigh simply me – all dressed up in a Santa-suit and a Santa-beard? Am I just looking at myself, in a mirror, as we ride along? Well I hope not – I don't think so – and yet there's nothing more creative – or more realistic-seeming – than a dream. Nothing more capable of manufacturing images – people and places – that one has never, in actual life, ever seen. The colour of his eyes – the shape of his nose – his body-language as he holds the reins – are either Santa or a character who is being created by me. Now what could I ask him that would prove that he isn't me?

The bright flame

The percentages of what one knows and doesn't know.
An orange or an apple in a stocking.
Whether or not to drink a glass of milk.

burns brightest

And what have you ever done that would equal Santa's contribution?
Has writing your books been the best use of your time?
Was there no humanitarian work that you could have done?

in the daylight.

Eastern feast day, December 19.
Left quite a bit of money by his parents.
Lives at the North Pole.

There's the Tooth Fairy, the Easter Bunny and Santa Claus, the little boy explained.
The night of darkness ending.
When we first started out, I pictured myself holding a handful of oats for Rudolph to chew, and rubbing him on the head, and patting him on the neck, and getting a close look at the nature of the famous red nose. And Santa would be aging – a little forgetful as time has

gone by – and telling charming stories, like the time he left his box-lunch instead of a present at a little boy's house. But somehow it hasn't turned out like that – not as cosy as I thought it would be – though Santa assures me that he also gives traditional tours.

"Why thank you my little lad. I didn't know that I had dropped it. I'll be more careful in future. I can't afford to be dropping money on the floor.

"I wouldn't have known if you had kept it. I was completely unaware. You are a very polite and kind little boy."

His mom and dad were seated further forward. His brother and sister were in the concert. He slid along past the knees and took his seat.

Resisting the temptation to reach out and pinch Santa.

Resisting the temptation to reach out and pinch myself.

I hover inside my computer-screen! I am floating in a cartridge of ink! I am searching for the exit! I need to be printed on a page! The printer will spit me onto the table or onto the floor!

The basis of all literature - no doubt in my mind - open the head - a deeply-troubled individual - how do i know - aware of the suffering - sometimes it's treasured - explaining a set of rules - a force in life - essentially a child's world.

Well, this Christmas doesn't look so good. It'll still be Christmas, for sure, but it'll be a little curtailed.

Covid 19 has put a crimp in what we all think of as the way to celebrate the holiday. It's been two years of restricted gatherings – all to try to break the back of the raging pandemic. Our book-discussion group used to meet every second Thursday of each month until Covid 19 came along, and since then we have only had three summer meetings, all outside, and only recently were we able to meet inside. So after two years of not meeting, we all wear masks to enter the room, we all show our vaccination certificates, we all sit six and a half feet apart and we don't have tea or coffee or anything to eat. And now this new variant, Omicron, is turning the whole world back to what it was. To gather in groups – as we always do at Christmas – is the worst thing during a pandemic that people can do.

He was looking
for his granddaughter.

Am I showing Santa my places or is he showing me? Are we taking trips to my former Christmases or am I only imagining that we are? Maybe I'm daydreaming as I ride along in the sleigh. Maybe the reality is that we're visiting all of Santa's places and none of my own.
If thou know'st it, telling.
Perhaps if my kids were along – at a time when they were still three little boys, and their mom would dress them up in matching sweaters and we'd take them to a mall to have their picture taken with Santa Claus. I don't regret this visit, of course – in fact I suspect that it's being tailored to suit my sensibility – but the other kind of tour would have been welcome – if my wife and three little boys had been along. I think I would have enjoyed it equally well.

Sorrowing, sighing, bleeding, dying.

Would it hurt Santa's feelings if I were to tell him that I'm becoming a trifle disappointed? When I thought of writing about him, I thought that he would probably be in touch with more of the mysteries of life – of the universe – than I now find that he seems to be. I had hoped to go – in novel-form – a league, a mile, a kilometer or two – beyond myself – in wisdom, in knowledge, in perception – beyond the known horizons – beyond the discovered stars. But I find that, although Santa isn't human, he's not a much-more privileged being than am I. I'm not sure, now, that I'll continue to think of writing about Santa at all. Perhaps – just perhaps – though I'll have to wait and see – I am a little more privileged than Santa. Perhaps I'll be told the secrets of the universe after I die. But Santa – immortal Santa – will be stuck forever here on Earth – with powers above a human, of course – but with no more knowledge of the universe than earthly I – and a lot less knowledge, perhaps, than I might be able to acquire, when all things are explained in the afterlife.

Each animal
was contributing
to the big red glow.

An entity – responding to its life-experience and thinking.

"We compile
separate lists, "
explained the Krampus.

Afternoon and the house was crowded. Thirty adults

and kids. Colour slides of the days when the adults were kids with new toys.

Presents and wrappings all over the floor. Laughing and sipping and chatting and singing along with the carols on TV. Turkey with gravy and everyone seated and bowing their heads.

The new scientific theory was that there could not be an experiment in which neither the scientist nor the subject of the experiment was not affected by the process in a major – or at least a subtle – way.

Commemorated in the Eastern and Western churches.
Gives gifts to help, not for praise.
He is one of the patron saints of sailors.

And they all take turns riding around the world in Santa's sleigh, the little boy added.
Flee from woe and danger.
We get so passionate in our dreams. So – one cowboy shirt went missing. There's another in a photograph. Perhaps I had shirt-after-shirt – with a cowboy motif – through all those years. Hard to see myself as 'deprived', or as 'a survivor' who is 'maimed-for-life' by 'post-traumatic essence-denial'. Hope Santa didn't think that I was overemphasizing the loss. Only a Gatsby could build a myth from a river of shirts.

"And what would you like for Christmas?" The hair was standing up on the head! The four-year-old looked down at his feet and murmured, "Twain"!

Walking along in the parking lot. "Well that was amazing to turn the corner and see Santa taking a break and eating a sandwich. We were surprised as much as he was surprised to see us."

Wondering why we are stopped in this little village. Riding with Santa is like watching the news on TV.

A large entity in a fur-trimmed suit! Black boots and a white beard! Exactly as everything should be! But there is something that disturbs me! I wonder where Santa is today!

To have any force - somewhere in your mind - the battle of the myths - the nature of how we think - ask a pertinent question - a dozen costumes inside - these under-ocean landmarks - myths that did not take hold - I would know them - decorate the house.

So my wife is getting ready. She has the house all decorated, as she always does – every year. She has invited our three sons and their families to come. Blake and his family make three. Adam and his family – three more. And Craig and his family make another four. Every day the rules are changing. Every night on the news it gets worse. They would be breaking into each other's circles of safety if they all came. Maybe, for safety, it's better that no one comes this year. If so, it will be my wife and I – as we were in Barbados that year. Just the two of us at Christmas-time again.

He raised his arm
and prepared to strike the final blow.

A bit of a bump this time. The first time our landing has not been smooth. I'm not so sure, but is this the first evidence of human habitation we have seen since we caught a glimpse of the workshop at the North Pole? It's amazing how ambivalent the reindeer seem. They drank water from the stream and munched the grass on the mountainside, but they never seem to actually need to rest or to refresh themselves. They just stop and wait until we are off again. Like the horse in the woods on a snowy evening – flick the ears a few times if you feel a flake of snow or a drop of rain. I can see wind in their coats and their noses seem wet, but I'm still not convinced that these are actual reindeer. I'd like to get a closer look at Rudolph's nose, but there's never been that kind of leisure time. We just sit in the sleigh and look at the various scenes. This one is a site of carnage on a massive scale.

Where they need no star to guide.

The streets are dust and cobblestones. The doors are all broken in. The roofs have been ripped off by some kind of siege-weapons, as most of them have caved right in. The wind blows dust in our faces, but it doesn't strike the eyes or the skin. There's a well that seems deserted – there is no movement in this town. Probably the well is filled with dust and battered debris. Broken bricks cover the pavement. I don't see broken glass at all. The rotting carcass of a donkey or a mule. Absolute destruction – hardly a stone left standing in place. I wonder what Santa is thinking. He sits and looks straight ahead. I can only wonder why he has brought me here. Not a person living or dead is here to be seen. The remnants of what once was a thriving community. You can see the stone where they used to grind the grain. Could be anywhere on this globe – could be anywhere across time. With these broken, time-worn columns, it's hard to tell whether this is contemporary Afghanistan or ancient Troy.

So what did the not-so-jolly elf want from this surprise-visitor – this unexpected-guest? For the visitor to write about him? – to change the way people think at Christmas-time?

Santa seems so absorbed in his thoughts. I wonder whether he noticed that I started my mother's family-Christmases a generation later than I did with my dad's. That was my father's family in Egremont – and my mom's family in Ospringe. My mother's father – my grandfather – Walter Davies – the Royal Marine – the one who poured the brandy and lit the Christmas-cake – was born in Barking – a suburb of London – in a room that was described in the report as 'sparse but clean'. So Christmases, for him, were probably not all that joyous. His father was a basket-weaver who couldn't earn enough to support his family, so after his wife died in childbirth, he offered four of his sons to the Barnardo homes.

In the bleak mid-winter.

I have a photo of my grandfather – Walter Davies – on the day that he was admitted to the orphanage – and a report from the inspector in Canada, where he was sent, that says that the boy has asked for ten dollars out of his six-year, one hundred dollar stipend to send to England to keep his father from being buried in a pauper's grave. It's a scene right out of Dickens. I don't think my mother ever knew – her father never told her – she thought that he was an orphan all those years.

Earth stood hard as iron.

But – on the other hand, if Santa is real – if this is the actual Santa, and not a creation of my imagination

– and if he is in charge of selecting these visions, rather than me – then perhaps he has made a conscious decision to keep the family Christmas-visits light, and avoid what could have been a painful scene.

There is only

Someone who is alone but never lonely.
Showing a present and saying a few words.
No fire on Christmas Eve.

what has been

And all those places that Santa is taking you?
What do you think he's trying to say?
Won't Santa be disappointed if you don't respond?

and what will always be.

So, explained the little boy, Rudolph visits my house – with the Easter Bunny, and the Tooth Fairy and Santa – at least three times every year.
Though the frost was cruel.
Does Santa visit these desolate places often, I wonder? Once in a life-time? – the span of a human life, that is – or once a year? Or just with me? – just this once – through a sense that these places are the ones where I would choose to go – if I had the use of Rudolph – and the sleigh – and the other eight tiny reindeer?

Chapter 9

Well John – you know how you like to take a break and buy a coffee and go for a drive. You like to park along the river – the Grand River, at Cayuga – and polish a chapter that you are working on. Or drive the country roads and sip your coffee and get an idea and pull over to the side of the road and scribble furiously at whatever occurs to you to write down. Well – I always see a lot of people on Christmas Eve. Christmas Eve will be here again in a few short days. Most of the children will be asleep, but I'll see them – every one – and I know who all of them are. An occasional child will see me – I always make sure of that – and I'll see all the adults as well, though they won't see me.

Thy candles shine so brightly.

But when I'm not surrounded by people – between engagements, as it were – I like to take the sleigh and the reindeer – and just go. Go to all these places that I am sharing with you right now. And I just sit in the sleigh and think – or I get out and go for a walk – let the reindeer drink if it's a shallow stream or graze in a grassy field. And I just think about the things that are on my mind – the things that please me and the things that most certainly don't.

The dark flame

A person taking a drive so he can think.
A Mother who decorates the whole house.
The Tooth Fairy, the Easter Bunny and Jack Frost.

burns brightest

A girl falls down through a rabbit-hole?
And is surprised by what she finds?
A broken watch scattered in pieces all over the floor?

in the night.

Drawn by eight reindeer.
Nikolaos of Myra.
Flies around the world.

What they are, I'll keep to myself. There's no need for you to know. That's why I'm not providing a commentary today. Just a whim on my part, I suppose you could say.
Sitting on Santa's lap.
It was a Santa-Claus convention.

My Godmother doesn't know me, he thought. She didn't know that it was me. We used to see her every week at the other church.

Sensing that Santa is seeing me as a kindred spirit.
Expecting the dam to break and all his thoughts to come pouring forth.

There are forces in the world.
What is the force that duels with Santa?

Should it grapple with Santa
In my Ballad of Santa Claus?

We do need seeds - everything about christmas - the deeper question - my lost heritage - compile separate lists - a dream vacation - set these images aside - edged even closer - communicate in images - the mythical enterprise.

I just don't want to let go of that memory – or vision – or apparition or whatever it was. We had a pond, and I had a snow-blower and I fixed up a set of lights so the kids could play hockey long after it got dark. They could put their skates on in the basement and clump up the wooden stairs and across the frozen lawn and skip out onto the ice and drop the puck and stick-handle and practice shooting into these two-by-four nets that I made. And they would invite their friends from school or church – many of the kids were the same – and play for hours out on the rink we had on our pond. And Christmas Day – after dinner – we parents were all in our late thirties and early forties in those days – our two families and our friends would all bring their skates and sticks and we would all go out on the rink and have a game of shinny – a dozen players or more, all flailing away, trying to put the old puck in the net. And years afterwards, I would find beat-up pucks in the long grass around the edge of the pond which had skipped off the rink and landed in the snow. But we always had lots of pucks – the girls would all play hockey too – or practice their figure-skating moves as the boys went whirling by.

She always wore
a cap of snowflakes.

I don't know who or what sent you along. I was given no warning and certainly no instructions at all. I was just as surprised as you that you were – suddenly – sitting here beside me in my sleigh.

Selecting the perfect Christmas tree.

To tell the truth, John, I'm not deviating at all. This is exactly what I was planning to do today. Just take the sleigh and the reindeer and go out for what you would call 'a coffee-drive'. Just a chance to think about things as the scenery goes by. Just a means of breaking away from the daily routine.

> *"So when you feel down,*
> *just think of Rudolph,"*
> *the mongoose was saying,*

This is the essence – the basis – the concept – the reason-for-being – of all art.

> *"I'm proposing*
> *that Santa and I*
> *share our information.*

He felt odd all Christmas day. A glass of wine to end the evening. They tucked the two boys into their beds.

That there was no such thing as a pure experiment at all.

Traditionally associated with the festival of Christmas.

The patron saint of children.

Lives with his wife.

Oh there will be plenty and plenty of people. I don't live my life alone. There's my wife back at the house – there's the elves back at the shop. Pretty soon I'll be busy delivering gifts again.

Wrapping Christmas presents on the bed.

Santas were lined up around the block, and they were checking everyone's I.D. at the door.

"Oh that wasn't really Santa," said the four-year-old. "That was just a boy-Santa. He had black hair sticking out from under his beard."

Wondering where we're going to go next.

Wondering what Santa is going to come right out and say.

All of these myths have murky origins.
Wouldn't want to just make stuff up.
Better to do the dogged research
For my Ballad of Santa Claus.

Yield enough of a plot - wondering what to write - actual loaves and fishes - all it amounted to - guiding my thoughts - just your size - didn't have any questions - there was the proof - the rules are changing - a few interesting thoughts.

And afterwards, when we finished skating, or snowshoeing or cross-country skiing through the trails that the kids and I had made through the woods, we would all come into the house – a couple of dozen of us or more – and I would put a few more logs on the fire and we would have hot chocolate or a beer or a glass of wine and watch the Queen give her Christmas message from Sandringham, or wherever she used to have Christmas with her family. And then there might be a hockey or a football game on TV and then gradually – as the evening wore on – the little ones would drop off to sleep on the rug in front of the stove and each family would pack up the presents and sort through their coats and hats and mittens on the bed and the tangle of boots at the kitchen door and go out in the brisk night air and warm up their frigid cars and wave good-bye and Merry Christmas and Happy New Year and we'd shiver and go back in the house and find for sure that they'd left a present or two or a hat or some mittens behind. And that's how we used to spend Christmas, at our house near Cayuga – in the house we still live in now – on the Christmas Days of those years so long-ago.

But the sword froze in his hand –
his arm refused to move.

Oh – the view is just fantastic. Here we are in outer-space. The reindeer stand and wait patiently in harness, though they don't seem tired. I assume there's no wind in outer-space, though I've never pinned that down. What do rockets thrust against if there isn't any air? Santa never seems to want to talk. He just sits and looks at these scenes. Not a comment – not a word. His lips are not grim or compressed. With that hat and that beard it's hard to tell if he's making a frown. Everywhere we go he just sits and says not a thing. When he talks, when we are flying, he often ignores what I have to say. Someone else should be here to prod him. I'm really not the type. I just watch the panther sleeping

– don't tend to poke him with a stick. Someone else might get him to talk – but it won't be me.

We all want some figgy pudding.

This is where the scientists like to set up their telescopes – on those earth-made satellites like those that glint in the distance. Way out here where the light is clean and clear and they can see. We used to go outside and watch the first Sputnik go by in the sky. Physicists, I assume they would be – or are they still called astronomers, I wonder? Maybe that's a term that we no longer use when we gaze at the sky. The light – we are told – goes far beyond our galaxy. It started all the way back at the moment when time began. All the way – so I assume – beyond whatever we Earthlings have managed to see so far. We still don't see any end to the cosmos. Or any shape that it might have – whether a sphere or a loop or whatever. And there's a beyond – we keep finding out – beyond the beyond. Imagine trying to be a physicist – making up theories about what we'll probably – maybe – someday find. Something outside the furthest 'outside' there could possibly be.

Or, perhaps, he was hoping for the visitor – the guest who had turned up, so suddenly, in his sleigh – to write about his Santa-thoughts without the visitor ever mentioning the jolly old elf. Perhaps the visitor would be moved, in future – if he could only interpret these images – squeeze this carbon into diamonds in his clenched fist – to write, in response to what he'd been shown, a whole series – a long shelf – of deeper books than he'd managed to write so far.

Every odyssey is a path

Counting the reindeer in the sky.
Selecting an item from the catalogue.
Post-cards with greetings from 1905.

whose stones

Heroes tumbling into adventures?
Being swept along on the raging currents of idea-streams?
Learning that the greatest challenge is finding their way back home?

are etched in braille.

I sit and ride beside Santa, wondering what this is all about. In a way, there's been lots of talking. Much has been said and much has been heard. But in another sense – in another dimension of thought – this has not been much of an interview at all. I get the feeling that the topic is not the topic. That he hasn't said what's been on his mind at all. He's not the jolly old elf of fable, that's for sure.

Deer making tracks in the snow.

So – this is all very interesting. These places are quite fascinating – they seem to be places of the extreme. The highest reach of the mountains. The deepest depths of the sea. The two poles – the North and the South. Even outer-space – that's a spectacular view of the earth from so far away. It takes my breath away whenever I see it. Santa must find it awesome as well, despite the fact that he lives in a different sphere. But – why is he leading me here? So far from what I think of – of what everyone thinks of – as the places where Santa would care to spend his time? Why not Santa's workshop? – or various children's houses as they anticipate his visit on Christmas Eve? Santa is always associated with people – not with the ends of the earth and beyond – those voids beyond the grasp of human reach. We have seen everything but people in the places we've seen on this tour. And why does Santa not talk about these places at all?

Arriving home for the holidays.

Only one Santa was allowed to enter the hall.

Chapter 10

Oh! – here I am! – pulling into the driveway! Back again – driving my car. Well that's the end – I guess – of Santa Claus – for me.

In his master's steps he trod.

I'm sure I didn't fall asleep at the wheel. Surely the car hasn't been driving itself. If I was asleep, I would have been sure to go off the road.

They divide the world

A person driving home in a car.
A dream that might not be a dream.
Thinking in non-human terms.

between them

Why couldn't you work for humanitarian causes? Are you not aware of the suffering that goes on? Are you indifferent to the agony that you see every day on the news?

to this day.

In Asia Minor, near modern Demre, Turkey.
The custom of giving gifts and sweets to children.

Drawings in Harper's Weekly.

Amazing how many thoughts a person can have in only a few miles. It's only two or three miles from the meeting-place to here. Or five or six kilometers, I guess we're supposed to say.

Lighting a cake soaked in brandy.

Well, the mind certainly works on many levels. We think on many levels at a single moment in time. You can think about baking a cake – or writing a book – and all the while your mind is driving your car.

He sat and watched the rest of the Christmas concert. He remembered a concert with a skit about Cinderella. He wondered if a Fairy Godmother could be a little boy.

Arriving home from our Christmas book-discussion meeting.

Thinking of all the topics that we discussed.

He had a theory
that the books
are all about us.

His defenseless opponent - never interact with each other - a new concept - zero in on the moment - container of shaped-belief - a person who uses logic - dressed them in matching sweaters - i can only wonder - a charming little book - seemingly unlimited powers.

That there is
no such thing as
'art for art's sake'

at all.

He was poking
with his magic stick
in the snow.

I don't think I'll ever be able to rival Charles Dickens. Don't think I'll ever make up an iconic story that will alter the nature of how we think at Christmas-time. Not the kind of writer to write that kind of book.
Let nothing you dismay.
I'll be glad to get myself back to *Shakespeare and Cleopatra*. That's where I'm on my safest ground. There's plenty of thought there to keep me occupied. Caesar and Antony built themselves an empire – Cleopatra built herself a myth. Then Shakespeare came along and shuffled the cards. And then – I came along and did it all over again.

"And don't ever
feel ashamed
of your shiny red nose."

That art is a level of the mind –
a level of thought about ourselves
and our experience –
that is so far down in our heads
that we are not always aware.

"I'm proposing that
we consolidate
our lists."

The younger boy was just a baby. He didn't have

any questions to ask. Everything about Christmas was fine with him.

> That art is the dredging-up of the images
> from the mind's deep core
> and arranging them on the table
> for all to see
> and think about
> in concrete form.

The legend of Sinterklaas.
Portly, jolly, white-bearded.
Illustrator Haddon Sundblum.

Wonder whether it'll snow for Christmas – only about two weeks away. Let's see – coffee cup to go in the garbage-pail in the garage. Check the mailbox – it's Thursday today. Bring my bag along with my notes – they're still in the car. Wonder where that photograph got to – the one of me in the cowboy shirt. Probably in the little wooden box Dad made when we were just kids.

Watching a Christmas movie on TV.

A myth is a pile of sand. We are all children on the beach. Every grain has a place in the little sand-castle. Then a wave comes and seems to sweep it all away. But the sand is always there. The sand is there after the children are called up to the cottage. It will be there long after all of us are gone. It will be shaped by the water and by the wind.

He almost let go of his young son's hand. Right there in the parking lot. He was amazed at the power of thought of the four-year-old mind.

This was the boy whose hair had stood on end as they rounded the corner. This was the boy who had looked at his feet and murmured 'twain'. The boy held his dad's hand firmly as they walked to the car.

Thinking of the idea-structure of the Dickens novella.

A guide presents the main character with various scenes.

Whether a film or a painting,
or a sculpture or a vase,
or a poem or a poetic novel
or a poetic play.

I can speculate - how ideas are processed - soothe the troubled waters - his fire had gone out - know what this place is - bubble of some kind - grapple all over the world - couldn't possibly tell me anything - the topic, of course - i have no crystal ball.

That art is the everyday image-process
that ebbs and flows
like magma
in the depths of the brain.

The Sun Conqueror
would live to fight, again, next year.

It should have been Aeschylus or Sophocles – a society about to crack. It should have been Shakespeare along in the sleigh – a deeply-troubled individual flails away. Or maybe Homer – worlds in tension – the clash of gods on a vast terrain.

The hopes and fears of all the years.

I'm sure that if I were a different person, I'd phone the local news. Tell them I spent some time with Santa. Tell them what Santa had to say. Be picked up by the Canadian national newscast. That would be picked up, in turn, by New York. Then the talk-shows – maybe a movie. How this guy was hosted by Santa – given a moment – an hour – or a day. Taken to all the farthest places of which we're aware. And that Santa told him – what? Just what – exactly – did Santa have to say?

The only journey

Advertisements which feature Santa Claus.
A person with a head full of thoughts.
A theory of what is outside the outside.

one can take

Aren't you the one who's always writing about the power of images?
Are these images not slapping you in the face?
Aren't you tempted to grit your teeth and pick up the sword?

is with the eyes.

Up the stairs and across the porch. Just a handle on the door. The doornail practically comes alive at Scrooge's approach.
Merry Christmas to you.
All it amounted to was John and Santa – an hour or two of talk. The topic was never the topic. Santa's secrets are Santa's secrets still. I didn't get him to open

up and spill the beans. No, I don't think there's a novel in this – no novel at all.

Three Books

John and Santa: The Cowboy Shirt:
a novella

As the writer, John Passfield, is driving home from a December book-discussion meeting and thinking about the Christmas topics that were discussed – in particular, Dickens, who wrote a novella which transformed the world's conception of Christmas – he suddenly finds himself sitting in a sleigh pulled by Rudolph and eight tiny reindeer. What an excellent opportunity to ask Santa about a seventy-year-old mystery – the mystery of the missing cowboy shirt.

The Making of John and Santa: The Cowboy Shirt:
a reflective journal

This journal records the author's reflections on the process of the crafting of the novella as it evolved through the stages of planning, writing, editing and polishing. It constitutes an effort to be as conscious as possible of the process whereby the single idea that suggested the topic of the novella was expanded into a complex work of art. Topics range from the nuts and bolts of novel-building to the nature of the novel as an art-form.

Planning John and Santa: The Cowboy Shirt:
a planning notebook

During the writing of the novella, the author kept a notebook which records the day-by-day development of the novella as it found its shape and style. The notebook reveals how a vast cluster of thoughts was sifted, selected, structured and polished into novella-form.

The Project

Together, this novella, journal and notebook comprise the thirtieth installment in an ongoing novel-writing project in which the author is exploring the concept of form and meaning in the novel, and of the novel as a form of expression in the 21st Century. All of the published journals and notebooks are available for free access at www.johnpassfield.ca.

About the Author

John Passfield was born in St. Thomas, Ontario, Canada, and continues to reside in Southern Ontario, near Cayuga, with his family. He is interested in exploring the development of the novel as an art-form in a search for a form for the poetic novel of our time. He has published almost thirty novels, and his planning notebooks and journals are available for free access on his website, johnpassfield.ca. *His novel John Passfield: Saturday Morning* was shortlisted for the ReLit award in 2022. He has posted more than one hundred readings on YouTube, each of which presents a passage from one of his novels and a comment on an aspect of the craft of novel-writing.

Novels by John Passfield

Grave Song
The Agony of Robert Chisholm

Jumbo
P. T. Barnum's Greatest Creation

Pinafore Park
The Swan Boat Incident

Water Lane
The Pilgrimage of Christopher Marlowe

Rain of Fire
The Ordeal of Conductor Spettigue

Victoria Day
The Fabric of the Community

The Wright Brothers
Flight is Possible

Leni Riefenstahl
The Valley of the Shadow

Out of the Park
The Cogitations of Babe Ruth

Raskolnikov
Murder with an Axe

Death Day
The Apology of Sergei Eisenstein

Einstein
Wonder

Geoffrey Chaucer
Canterbury Bound

Ospringe
A Visit with Grandad

Pompeii
Vesuvius Dominus

Beethoven
The Ninth Immersion
Job
The Cornerstone of the Universe

Bethune
The Only Person Alive in the World

Terry Fox
Somewhere the Hurting Must Stop

Lord and Lady Macbeth
Full of Scorpions is My Mind
Cyril Passfield
Out West

Glenn Gould
Light and Dark

Emily Brontë
More Myself Than I

L. M. Montgomery
I Gave You Life

Pauline Johnson
Know Who I Am

John Passfield
Saturday Morning

Eleonora Duse
Let Me Have My Wings

James McIntyre
The Mammoth Cheese

Shakespeare and Cleopatra
My Life Is Not My Own

John and Santa
The Cowboy Shirt

John and Cassandra
Fair is Fair

John and Dickens
A Christmas Mystery

See www.johnpassfield.ca for publishing information.

In Search of Form and Meaning: Journals by John Passfield

Each journal is a day-by-day record of the complex process that a writer undergoes while crafting a work of art. It records the largest decisions, of structure and theme, and the smallest decisions, such as the choice of one word over another, and the constant interaction between the two. Each journal is a record of a writer's reflection on the craft of novel-writing.

The Making of Grave Song

The Making of Jumbo

The Making of Pinafore Park

The Making of Water Lane

The Making of Rain of Fire

The Making of Victoria Day

The Making of Flight is Possible

The Making of The Valley of the Shadow

The Making of Out of the Park

The Making of Murder with an Axe

The Making of Death Day

The Making of Wonder

The Making of Canterbury Bound

The Making of Ospringe

The Making of Vesuvius Dominus

The Making of The Ninth Immersion

The Making of The Cornerstone of the Universe

The Making of The Only Person Alive in the World

The Making of Somewhere the Hurting Must Stop

The Making of Full of Scorpions is My Mind

The Making of Out West

The Making of Glenn Gould: Light and Dark

The Making of Emily Brontë: More Myself Than I

The Making of L. M. Montgomery: I Gave You Life

The Making of Pauline Johnson: Know Who I Am

The Making of John Passfield: Saturday Morning

The Making of Eleonora Duse: Let Me Have My
Wings

The Making of James McIntyre: The Mammoth
Cheese

The Making of Shakespeare and Cleopatra: My Life Is
Not My Own

The Making of John and Santa: The Cowboy Shirt

The Making of John and Cassandra: Fair is Fair

The Making of John and Dickens: A Christmas
Mystery

See www.johnpassfield.ca for free access.

The Novel as an Art-Form:
Planning Notebooks
by John Passfield

Each planning notebook records the planning, writing, editing and polishing of each novel. Each notebook is an attempt to understand and organize the vast cluster of thoughts which occur as one grapples with the various levels of organization which a clear yet complex work of art demands.

Planning Grave Song

Planning Jumbo

Planning Pinafore Park

Planning Water Lane

Planning Rain of Fire

Planning Victoria Day

Planning Flight is Possible

Planning The Valley of the Shadow

Planning Out of the Park

Planning Murder with an Axe

Planning Death Day

Planning Wonder

Planning Canterbury Bound

Planning Ospringe

Planning Vesuvius Dominus

Planning The Ninth Immersion

Planning The Cornerstone of the Universe

Planning The Only Person Alive in the World

Planning Somewhere the Hurting Must Stop

Planning Full of Scorpions is My Mind

Planning Out West

Planning Glenn Gould: Light and Dark

Planning Emily Brontë: More Myself Than I

Planning L. M. Montgomery: I Gave You Life

Planning Pauline Johnson: Know Who I Am

Planning John Passfield: Saturday Morning

Planning Eleonora Duse: Let Me Have My Wings

Planning James McIntyre: The Mammoth Cheese

Planning Shakespeare and Cleopatra: My Life Is Not My Own

Planning John and Santa: The Cowboy Shirt

Planning John and Cassandra: Fair is Fair

Planning John and Dickens: A Christmas Mystery

See www.johnpassfield.ca for free access.

Other Books
by John Passfield

Oak Street
The Passfield Family

The Poetic Novel I
Influences and Elements

Intensities I
(1–100)
Verses on Various Topics

Intensities II
(101–200)

Intensities III
(201–300)

Intensities IV
(301–400)

Deepening Imagery I
(1—103)
Verses from the Novels

Deepening Imagery II
(104–200)

Deepening Imagery III
(201–214)

See www.johnpassfield.ca for free access.

www.ingramcontent.com/pod-product-compliance
Lightning Source LLC
Chambersburg PA
CBHW011044190726
48290CB00011B/2986